MILLERSBURG ELEMENTARY SCHOOL
P. O. BOX 238
MILLERSBURG, IN 46543

2nd grade

PATRICK

and

TED

PATRICK

and

TED

Geoffrey Hayes

SCHOLASTIC INC.

ISBN 0-590-40436-9

12 11 10 9 8 7 6 5 4 3 2 1   6 7 8 9/8

Printed in the U.S.A.

For Kal,
and the memory of "Racer"

Patrick and Ted went everywhere together.
Their favorite place was beneath a big
tree in Patrick's backyard.

They spent whole mornings there,
building hideouts and sharing secrets.

Sometimes they argued over toys, or about which games to play,

but it did not matter...

because Ted was Patrick's best friend,
and Patrick was Ted's.

They were like brothers, and nobody ever thought of one without thinking of the other.

Then, one summer Ted went to stay
with his aunt and uncle at
their farm in the hills.

After he left, Patrick had no one to build
things with, no one to tell secrets to.

But as the days went by,

he began to play with the other kids and
found that he enjoyed being just Patrick.

He went to the movies with Mama Bear.

He made a rocket ship
from soap cartons.

He rode his new scooter to a hideout
of his own.

In the fall, Ted returned with two pet
geese, a present from his aunt and uncle.

They were loud and quick, and Patrick
did not like them.

Patrick showed Ted his new scooter and how
to make it zoom around corners. But
Ted grabbed it away from him.

Patrick got angry and pushed Ted
against their hideout.

Patrick and Ted fixed their hideout
and spent the rest of the morning
playing games and sharing secrets.

From that day on, Patrick and Ted
no longer did everything together,
but it did not matter,

because Ted was still Patrick's best friend,
and Patrick was Ted's.